THEY SAY
BLUE

JILLIAN TAMAKI

ABRAMS BOOKS FOR YOUNG READERS
NEW YORK

They say blue is the
color of the sky.

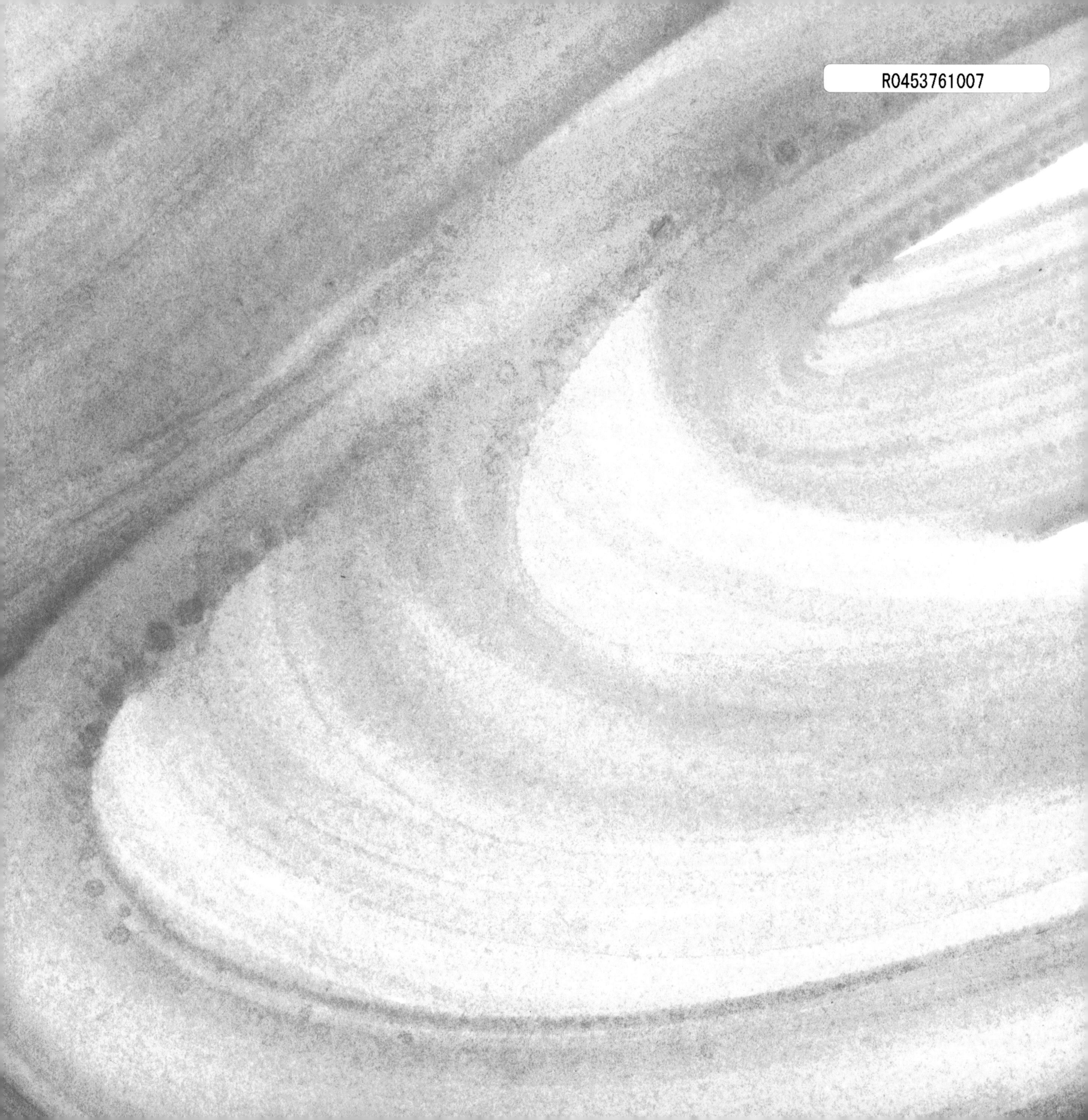

Which is true today! They say the sea is blue, too.

It certainly looks
like it from here.

But when I hold the
water in my hands, it's
as clear as glass.

I toss it up in the air to make diamonds.

What about a blue whale?
Is a blue whale blue?

I don't know.
I've never seen a blue
whale . . .

. . . but I don't need to crack
an egg to know it holds an
orange yolk inside.

I can't see my blood,
but I know it's red. It moves
around my body even when
I am perfectly still.

And when we play,
I feel it race faster
to keep up.

A field of grass looks
like a golden ocean.

If I built a boat that was
light enough, maybe
I could sail upon it.

Gray clouds.
A storm is coming.

I could never build a boat
light enough to sail on a
golden ocean.

It's just plain old yellow
grass anyway.

They say spring means winter's over, but why does it still feel so cold?

Oh!
Could purple mean
something new?

It's warm at last.

I stretch to the sky
with my fingers
open wide.

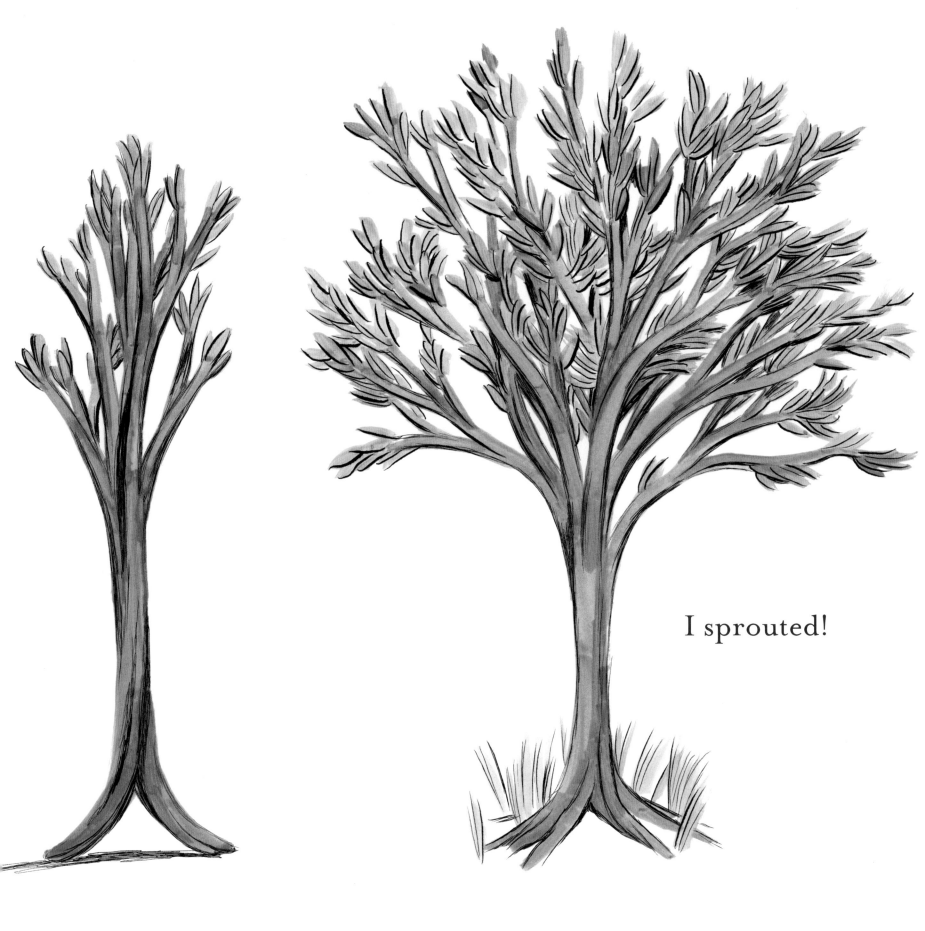

I sprouted!

Standing tall, I angle my green
leaves to feel the sun.
I think I'll stay quiet and listen to
the sounds of the summer.

Fall arrives, and my leaves slowly turn brown. I drop them one by one and wiggle my toes in the soft pile at my feet.

Winter's come again.
Now the rest of the world
is quiet, too.

All white, up and down.
Sometimes I can't tell the
difference between the
land and sky.

I close my eyes.

Oh, I'm so sleepy . . .

Black is the color
of my hair.

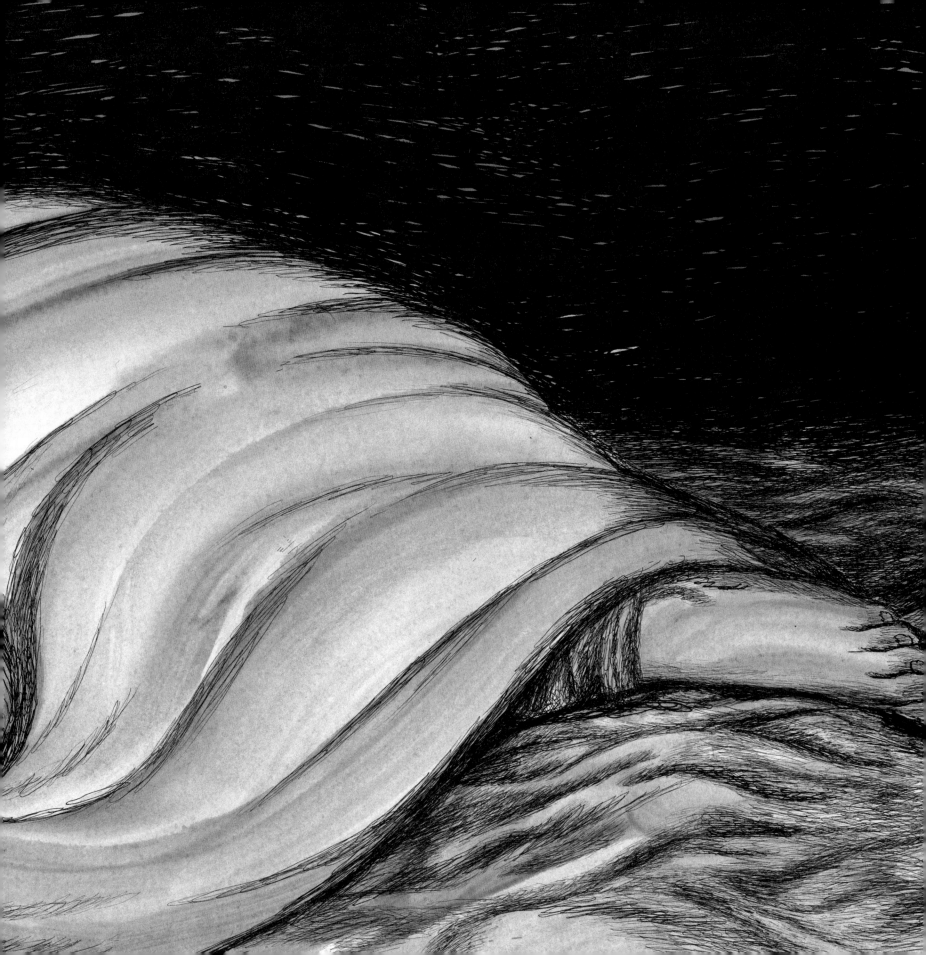

My mother parts it
every morning, like
opening a window.

Together we watch the
black crows bob
and chatter in the
field outside.

We wonder what
they are thinking
when they look at us.
What they see.

Their dark eyes
won't tell.

They just pull their
big bodies into the air.

Tiny inkblots on
a sea of sky.

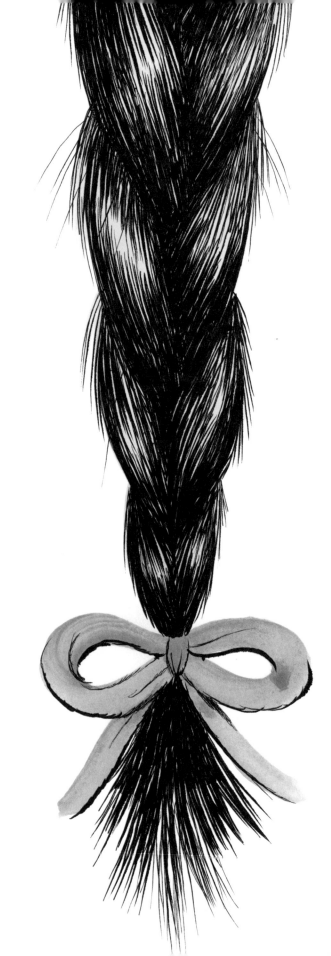

For my parents

THE ILLUSTRATIONS IN THIS BOOK
WERE MADE WITH A COMBINATION
OF ACRYLIC PAINT ON WATERCOLOR
PAPER AND PHOTOSHOP.

Cataloging-in-Publication Data has been
applied for and may be obtained from
the Library of Congress.

ISBN 978-1-4197-2851-8

Text and illustrations copyright
© 2018 Jillian Tamaki
Book design by Jillian Tamaki
and Chad W. Beckerman

Printed and bound in U.S.A.
13 12 11 10 9 8 7 6 5 4

Abrams Books for Young Readers are available at
special discounts when purchased in quantity for
premiums and promotions as well as fundraising
or educational use. Special editions can also
be created to specification. For details, contact
specialsales@abramsbooks.com or the address below.

ABRAMS The Art of Books
195 Broadway, New York, NY 10007
abramsbooks.com